Wakefield Libraries
& Information Services

2 8 SEP 2013

1 9 MAR 2016

1 5 SEP 2023

This book should be returned by the last date stamped above. You may renew the loan personally, by post or telephone for a further period if the book is not required by another reader.

Two Naughty Angels

Round the Rainbow

Mary Hooper

Illustrated by Lesley Harker

BLOOMSBURY

First published in Great Britain in 1997 by Bloomsbury Publishing Plc
36 Soho Square, London, W1D 3QY

This edition first published in 2008

A CIP catalogue record of this book is available from the
British Library

ISBN 978 0 7475 9062 0

All papers used by Bloomsbury Publishing are natural, recyclable products made
from wood grown in well-managed forests. The manufacturing processes conform
to the environmental regulations of the country of origin.

Typeset by Dorchester Typesetting Group Ltd
Printed in Great Britain by Clays Ltd, St Ives Plc

1 3 5 7 9 10 8 6 4 2

www.bloomsbury.com
www.maryhooper.co.uk

Prologue

Angels are always bright and beautiful, but they are also sometimes BORED. That's why Angela and Gabrielle, who have been in heaven for two hundred and fifty years, jump through the magic viewing mirror and come to earth.

They land in St Winifred's Convent School for Girls, where only Julia, their best friend, knows they're angels. The very important and magnificent Archangel keeps showing up in earthly mirrors and trying to get them back to heaven, but our angels have no intention of going. Not for all the feathers in a wing!

Everything is working out well for Angie and Gaby until the day they despatch a ghost from earth, and one of their teachers, Sister Bertha, gets sent to heaven by mistake!

Now our naughty angels have to try to put things right . . .

A Flying Start

Gaby wriggled her wings, opened them out fully and rose a few feet into the air.

'Oh, that's better! It's so nice to stretch your wings,' she said.

Angie fluttered hers and joined Gaby halfway up a tree. 'It is, isn't it?' she said. 'It does them no good at all to be squashed under a vest all day.'

Gaby and Angie had come out to the school field to have a bit of a fly around – and also to decide what to do about Sister Bertha, a teacher at their school who'd gone to heaven before her time.

'Well, it wasn't *our* fault,' Angie said. 'We didn't know Sister Bertha would come into our dorm just when the guardian angel appeared, did we?'

'It doesn't matter whose fault it was,' Gaby said gloomily, 'Sister Bertha is where she shouldn't be and we're going to get into awful trouble' – she pointed upwards – '*you know where.*'

'Upstairs in the dorms?' Angie asked.

'Upstairs in heaven, silly!' Gaby said. 'What do you think the Archangel is going to say about someone arriving from earth who isn't dead? It's strictly against the rules.'

'Well,' Angie said earnestly, 'can't we just explain to him that we sent the school ghost back to heaven where she belonged . . .'

'Back to a lower level than *ours*, of course!' put in Gaby, who was a bit snobbish about ghosts.

'And then just explain to him that Sister Bertha

accidentally went too,' Angie continued.

'That's as may be,'
Gaby said, as she
reached up to take
an apple from the
branch, 'but the fact
is we've messed up
the right order of
things and he's going
to be *very cross*.'

Angie nodded thoughtfully. 'I suppose if it
hadn't been for our heavenly singing, Sister Bertha
wouldn't have come up in the middle of the night
and found us.' She sighed. 'We're *never* going to get
our haloes back now!'✻

'I never had one in the first place,' said Gaby –
who was rather naughtier than Angie.

Angie gave a smug smile. 'Well, you never went
to Halo Awareness Classes, did you?'

✻ Angels have to earn their haloes – the better they
are, the brighter the haloes.

'The other thing,' Gaby went on, taking no notice of the dig, 'is that now the Archangel will be even more determined to get us back to heaven.'

'Oh *no*!' Angie sighed again. 'Just think what it should be like if we had to go back: no more television . . .'

'No more animals . . .'

'No more proper food . . .'

'No more midnight feasts . . .'

'No more fun!'

'And what would we get instead?' Gaby groaned. 'Just a whole lot of clouds!' She gave a vast sigh and a few drops of rain fell.

Both angels looked up to the sky. 'Oops,' Angie said. 'We've both been sighing.'✳

'We'd better go in,' Gaby said. 'I hate getting my wings wet.'

'And my ringlets go all frizzy! But what shall we do about Sister Bertha?'

'I think we'll just sit tight and see,' Gaby said.

✳ When angels sigh, storm clouds gather and rain falls.

'Maybe no one will realise she isn't here. Maybe they'll just think she's gone on holiday.'

The angels landed gently on the grass, tucked in their wings and began to walk back to school.

'I don't want to go back to heaven,' Gaby said. 'I'm not ready.'

Angie thought for a moment. 'Nor am I,' she said. 'I wasn't sure at first about coming down here, but now I really like it.'

'I might be ready to go back in a hundred and fifty years or so,' Gaby said, 'but right now I'm enjoying myself too much.'

They went into school – and bumped straight into their form teacher, Miss Bunce.

Miss Bunce was an old dear who'd been at St Winifred's for years and years. She was one of the few teachers who wasn't a nun. Instead of wearing black, she wore a strange assortment of floaty dresses, wispy scarves and brightly coloured shawls. The whole effect was that of a small walking tent.

'Dears!' she said to Gaby and Angie. 'Mother

Superior has called a special meeting in the school hall, and every girl and every teacher has to attend. Run along and tell the other First Years, will you?'

Gaby and Angie nodded politely, but Gaby angel-whispered to Angie, 'What if the meeting's about Sister Bertha?!'✻

Angie gave a small shriek of alarm.

'Er . . . what's the meeting about?' Gaby asked Miss Bunce.

'We'll find that out in good time,' Miss Bunce said gently. 'Now, off you go, because Mother Superior wants us there immediately. I'm going up to Sister Bertha's study to tell her about it. Come to think of it, I haven't seen Sister Bertha for

✻ Angels can speak to each other so softly no one else can hear.

a day or so,' she murmured as she wandered off.

Gaby and Angie looked at each other.

'Oh *no*!' Gaby said. 'She's going to find out that Sister Bertha's disappeared.'

'So what shall we do now?'

Gaby thought for a moment. 'Come on!' she said, tugging Angie. 'We're going to have to get a bit wet – but it's all in a good cause.'

'Where are we going?'

'Sister Bertha's room!'

Once outside, the angels flapped their wings and in a few seconds had flown up to Sister Bertha's third-floor study. The window, luckily, was open, and they slipped inside.

'Now what?' Angie said. 'Miss Bunce will be here in a minute.'

'We're going to play Sister Bertha!' Gaby said.

8

'*What?!*'

'Well,' Gaby said. 'Miss Bunce is coming up here expecting to see Sister Bertha, so one of us is going to pretend to be her.'

There was a moment's silence.

'Goodbye,' Angie said as she headed for the door.

'It's OK,' Gaby said. 'I'll do it. You go outside in the corridor and warn me when she's coming.'

Eyes wide with fright, Angie did as she was told. Gaby looked round the room, found Sister Bertha's spare black habit on the back of the door and put it on, fitting the starched white head-covering around her face.

She picked up the long skirt and went to the door. 'How do I look?' she asked.

Angie giggled. 'All right,' she said, 'but it's miles too long for you!'

'Watch this, though,' Gaby said, and she went back into the room and stood by the window with her face turned away. Because the habit fell from her head right down her back, there was room for her wings to flap, and when she did this she rose into the air and was as tall as Sister Bertha!

'Clever!' Angie said admiringly. 'But how are you –' She suddenly broke off. 'She's coming!' she said. 'I'm going!'

A moment later Miss Bunce knocked and came into the room. 'Sister Bertha?' she asked gently. 'Are you quite well?'

'Atishoo!' Gaby sneezed.

'Oh, I wondered . . . I thought I hadn't seen you all day. There's a meeting in the school hall, but if you're not well enough . . .'

Gaby sneezed again, so loudly and violently that she surprised herself. ✻

'You do sound dreadful,' Miss Bunce said. 'Let me make a you a hot drink.'

✻ Angels are never ill. They don't even have colds, so they never sneeze.

'Miss Bunce!' Angie called from outside. 'Is it *now* that everyone's got to go to the hall? I couldn't remember if it was now or tomorrow.'

Miss Bunce tutted gently. 'Silly child,' she said, 'of course it's now. And we've got to hurry!' She turned back to the black-robed figure. 'I should have an early night, Sister Bertha. See you in the morning.'

The second the door had closed behind Miss Bunce, Gaby fluttered to the floor.

Having wings comes in *very* handy, she thought.

2

Save Our School!

The whole of St Winifred's had gathered to hear their head teacher, Mother Superior, speak. The First Year girls were at the front of the hall, and the seven girls who slept in the tower dorm – Angie and Gaby, Julia, Nicola, Susie, Sarah and Marcy – were in the first row.

Mother Superior was standing on the stage looking as serious as a very short, fat nun with pink-striped socks and ankle boots *could* look.

'Now, girls,' she said, looking at the classes ranged down the hall. 'I have something very important to say to you. St Winifred's has been here a long, long time. For years we have been helping girls on their paths to womanhood. Now all that is in jeopardy.'

'Where's jeopardy?' Angie angel-whispered to Gaby.

'Ssshhh! It means in *danger*,' Gaby said.

Mother Superior paused, and one hundred and eighty girls, two angels and the staff of the convent, right down to the cook and gardener, looked back at her inquiringly.

'St Winifred's, our dear school,' said Mother Superior, 'is, I am afraid to say, in severe financial difficulties.'

A gasp broke out across the hall.

'Not to put too fine a point on it, we are absolutely stony broke. Unless we can somehow get more money, we shall have to close the school at the end of this term.'

A buzz of conversation started amongst the girls, and Mother Superior clapped her hands for silence. 'I have composed a song, a very sad song, to mark this occasion, and I'd like to sing it to you now.'

Everyone in the hall exchanged secret, horrified glances. Mother Superior was famous for her singing, which was so bad that Matron had got in a year's supply of earplugs and gave them out on request. Unfortunately, no one had been expecting a song today, so no one had earplugs at the ready.

Mother Superior went to the side of the stage, picked up her guitar and began strumming.

'It isn't very funny,
We don't have any money,
We don't have any money,
No, we don't.'

She roared the words tunelessly, and from the side of the hall Stanley, the gardener's dog, who'd come with his master, set up a pitiful howling.

'Is Stanley saying something?' asked Julia, the angels' best friend and the only person on earth who knew they were angels. 'Or is he just howling?'*

H-O-O-O-O-OWL

'He said he really can't stand that noise,' Gaby said.

'And if it keeps up he's going to join a circus,' Angie put in.

'If you could keep your dog quiet,' Mother Superior said to the gardener, 'I shall continue with the next ten verses.'

As the girls groaned under their breath, Stanley howled again, then gave a *wuff-wuff-wuff*.

'He says there's a rabbit outside and he wants to chase it,' Gaby whispered to Julia.

Suddenly Stanley tore out, taking the gardener with him, and Mother Superior carried on singing.

* Angels can understand and speak the language of animals.

15

By the time she'd finished, everyone in the hall was feeling quite ill.

She put down her guitar and looked at the girls. 'Now, can anyone suggest a solution to this awful problem?'

Angie stood up. 'Please, you could have singing lessons.'

Mother Superior smiled grimly. 'I mean a solution to the problem of the school closure.'

'Oh,' Angie said, and sat down again.

Sister Anne rose to her feet. She was a young, rather serious nun who took the girls for Music and Drama.

'Mother Superior,' she said, 'I may have the answer. I've been contacted by one of the television companies to ask if we have anyone of outstanding singing talent who'd like to enter an inter-school competition.'

Mother Superior beamed. 'Of course! I shall be pleased to enter. I shall compose a new song!'

'No, no,' Sister Anne said, flustered. 'It's for *pupils*. Twelve schools are to take part and the television company will come to the school to televise each act. The singer – or singing group – voted the winner will receive a very large sum of money for her school.'

Mother Superior, looking slightly disgruntled, said, 'And you have a girl in mind for this, do you?'

'I have two girls in mind,' said Sister Anne. 'Two girls of outstanding singing ability.'

Girls throughout the school began to nudge each other, wondering who she was talking about, but the First Year girls knew all right, and looked at Angie and Gaby, who had such pure, sweet voices that they could literally sing the birds off the trees.

Gaby and Angie tried to look surprised and modest, but even in heaven they'd been called upon to do solos, so they knew they were absolutely glorious compared to anyone on earth.

Miss Bunce spoke up proudly. 'I presume you are talking of my First Year girls, Gabrielle and Angela.'

'I am,' Sister Anne said. 'They have extraordinarily beautiful voices. They haven't been at school long but I've been monitoring their progress carefully. I've rather taken them under my wing.'

'Didn't know she had one!' Gaby whispered, and the girls around her laughed – though they didn't know half the joke.

'And perhaps,' Mother Superior said, 'while the television people are at our school, they might discover a rather talented Mother Superior!'

'Yes, but what a pity we don't know one,' Angie said, and there were more giggles from the front of the hall.

Luckily, Mother Superior didn't hear. She beamed at Gaby and Angie.

'I don't want to put too much of a burden on those small shoulders,' she said, 'but just let me say that the whole future of St Winifred's depends on you!'

Gaby and Angie exchanged looks. 'Ah well,' Gaby angel-whispered, 'at least those two hundred and fifty years in the heavenly choir did us some good!'

When they left the hall all the First Year girls went into their common room and crowded round Gaby and Angie, pleased that the two girls were going to represent the school.

All except Marcy.

Marcy had been suspicious of the angels ever since they'd arrived at school. She'd stolen things from their dorm and tried to blame it on them. She'd tried to catch them out in the showers, too — finding it very strange that no one ever saw them without their vests. And as well as being nasty to them, she was forever asking them awkward questions.

'You two are *always* the centre of attention,' she said spitefully. 'I don't know what's so special about you, I'm sure. You're so pleased with yourselves, aren't you – with your silly golden curls and your wonderful voices!'

Before Gaby could think of a reply, Miss Bunce came in, her scarves all of a quiver.

'I've had such a shock,' she said. 'I've just discovered that Sister Bertha has gone missing! She's completely disappeared! Oh, what a calamity!'

3

Nun-napped!

Gaby and Angie stared at Miss Bunce.

'I thought you went up to see her earlier – when you left us,' Gaby said innocently. 'Wasn't she there?'

'I *thought* I'd seen her,' Miss Bunce said in a shocked voice, 'but it was someone *pretending* to be her. I went upstairs to her study again after our meeting in the hall, and found her habit and gown on the floor in a crumpled heap. I realise now that I didn't really see her at all!'

'Do you think she's been kidnapped?' Nicola

asked excitedly.

'Nun-napped!' Gaby said.

'Hush, child!' Miss Bunce said, outraged. 'That isn't even slightly amusing. Now, I want every one of you to rack your brains. Has anyone seen Sister Bertha?' No one replied and she went on, 'Come on. Someone *must* have seen her.'

Angie put up her hand. 'I've seen her!'

Gaby sighed under her breath. Angie just couldn't forget she was an angel, could she? She *always* had to tell the truth.

'Yes, Angela,' Miss Bunce said. 'And where have you seen her?'

'Everywhere!' Angie said. 'In class, out of class. In the dining hall, in chapel, in the playground, in the gym, in the –'

Miss Bunce tutted. 'Thank you, dear,' she said. 'I think we've all seen Sister Bertha going about her normal teaching duties around the school. What I mean is, has anyone seen Sister Bertha since she disappeared?'

'How could anyone do that?' Angie asked, shaking her ringlets in puzzlement. 'How could anyone have seen her since she disappeared? If they'd seen her, she couldn't have disappeared, could she?'

'Oh, do sit down, dear,' Miss Bunce said.

As Angie sat, Gaby frowned at her. 'Don't say anything else,' she angel-whispered. 'Not another thing! If they find out we had anything to do with Sister Bertha disappearing, we're going to get into big trouble. You know what Julia told us when we first got here – that if anyone ever suspects we're not real girls we'll be taken away and *investigated*.'

'But I can't tell lies!' Angie said.

'You don't have to tell lies. Just don't tell the truth. Don't say *anything*.'

'But –'

'Ssshh!' Gaby said sternly.

'Now I come to think of it,' Miss Bunce went on, 'I last saw Sister Bertha, the real Sister Bertha, on Saturday evening at midnight. She told me she'd heard singing coming from the tower dorm, and was going up to see what was happening. She said that the singing – and dear Sister Bertha is always a

23

bit fanciful, of course – sounded like a heavenly choir of angels.'

Gaby and Angie hid their giggles. Sister Bertha hadn't been fanciful. It had sounded like angels singing because it *was* angels singing. The two of them had sung 'Angels from the Realms of Glory' to summon their guardian angel, who would take the school ghost away, not dreaming that she'd whisk Sister Bertha into heaven as well.

'Now, I want all you First Years – and the girls in the tower dorm especially – to try and remember if anything strange happened last Saturday. Did anyone see Sister Bertha? I will give you two min- utes to talk amongst yourselves . . .'

The girls formed little whispering groups.

'We can't tell Miss

Bunce,' Julia said, 'but that was the night we had the midnight feast. We were all up and awake.'

'I wasn't!' Marcy said sourly. 'I slept right through the feast and didn't wake up until ten o'clock the next morning.'

'I wonder why that was?' Gaby said innocently.

'Oh, Gaby, don't you remember?' Angie said. 'We sprink—'

Gaby gave Angie a glare. 'Ssh!' she angel-whispered. 'Of course I remember. We sprinkled angel dust on her pillow so she wouldn't wake up.' *

'So Sister Bertha said she was going up to our dorm, did she?' Sarah asked with a frown. 'No one mentioned this before. Perhaps one of us *does* know something. You *were* asleep the whole time, weren't you, Marcy?'

'Yes, I was,' Marcy said. 'If I *had* woken up I'd have come and joined you downstairs.'

'We were all together, then,' Sarah said. 'We

* Angels always have angel dust in their pockets, just in case they have to send cherubs off to sleep.

went downstairs together, had the feast and then came back up together.'

'And I missed it all,' Marcy muttered darkly. 'What I want to know is, who was pretending to be Sister Bertha?'

'Never mind that now,' Sarah said. She turned to Gaby and Angie. 'But you two went back to the dorm in the middle of everything, didn't you?' she said. 'I remember you went to fetch some more food. Did you see Sister Bertha?'

'Yes, we —'

'No!' Gaby interrupted Angie swiftly.

Angie looked at Gaby, eyes wide. 'You mustn't tell lies!' she angel-whispered. 'At Halo Awareness Classes we always say, *If an angel tells a lie, You will see a flower die.*'

'Sometimes,' Gaby angel-whispered back, 'a little bit of a lie is necessary. Now, be quiet!' She smiled sweetly at Sarah. 'We didn't see anything,' she said to her. 'Not a thing!'

On a window sill in the common room a large pink rose suddenly lost all its petals.

'See!' Angie pointed. 'Told you!'

'Hmm,' Sarah said. 'I just can't understand it. I mean, Sister Bertha can't have vanished into thin air, can she?'

'No, she could have vanished into a mirror, though!' Gaby angel-whispered to Angie.

Miss Bunce clapped her hands. 'Now, girls,' she said. 'Has anyone got any ideas about what might have happened?'

Gaby gave a Angie a look, and Angie put her hands tightly over her ears so that she wouldn't have to hear Miss Bunce asking any questions.

The rest of the girls shook their heads or murmured that they had absolutely no idea where Sister Bertha had gone.

'Well, this was our last hope,' Miss Bunce said. 'The school and grounds have already been searched. Now Mother Superior will have to call in the police. We must find out what's happened to Sister Bertha!'

'Perhaps she's gone on holiday,' Gaby suggested, and added in angel-whisper to Angie, 'she's certainly taken a late flight somewhere.'

'A holiday is hardly likely,' Miss Bunce said. She looked at her girls rather sternly. 'I can't help feeling that some of you may know more than you're saying. Sister Bertha told me she was going up to the tower dorm, so it's the girls who sleep there who will be spoken to first. There will be *investigations*.'

Miss Bunce swept out, shawls swaying, leaving Gaby and Angie looking at each other in dismay.

'What . . . what's a police?' Angie asked, and as the others looked at her strangely, added, 'We don't have them in hea—'

'They don't have them where Angie and Gaby come from – in Nevaeh,' Julia said quickly, 'because there's no crime there.'

She turned to Angie, 'Police look into crimes – the bad things people do. Or they hunt for missing people, like Sister Bertha. They investigate.'

Angie had only picked up on one word. 'Investigate,' she said. 'They're going to *investigate* us. Oh *no*.'

⭐ Nevaeh is heaven spelt backwards, so if our angels say they come from there, it's not really a lie.

4

More Dead Flowers!

Gaby and Angie were sitting with Julia up in their dorm. They were supposed to be tidying themselves before supper but, as it's very difficult for an angel to look anything but radiant and glorious anyway, they were just sat chatting. The school cats, Tiblet and Felix, were on their laps.

'So much has happened today!' Julia said. 'First we're told that St Winifred's is broke, then we hear about the talent competition, now we find out that Sister Bertha is missing.' She tickled Tiblet under his chin. 'Where's Sister Bertha gone then, Tiblet?'

she asked idly. 'Bet you know and you're not telling.'

Tiblet meowed several times. Gaby and Angie looked at each other and grinned.

'Good job only we understood that!' Gaby said.

'What did he say?' Julia asked.

'He said that a bright light came out of our bathroom mirror and that Sister Bertha went into it!' said Gaby.

Julia's jaw dropped 'Well!' she said. 'I might have known you had something to do with it. Where's she gone, then?'

'She's gone to heaven,' Angie said.

Julia gasped. 'You mean she's dead?'

'Oh no,' Gaby said. 'She's gone before her time. It was all a mistake.'

'So what are you going to do?' Julia asked.

'Well,' Gaby replied, 'it's an awful drag, but it looks like we're just going to have to go to heaven and get her back.'

'You're not!' Julia flopped backwards on her bed in amazement. Tiblet jumped off her and went to Angie. 'But how will you get there? And I thought your Archangel wanted you back in heaven. If you get up there, won't he make you stay?'

'He might try,' Gaby said.

Julia pulled a face. 'You will come back, won't you?' she asked anxiously. 'It wouldn't be the same here without you.' She tickled Angie's back, where her wings folded. 'I love being the only girl in the world with angels for friends.'

'Of course we'll come back!' Gaby said. 'We promise.' She added thoughtfully, 'I suppose we'll have to get back here the same way we came — through the viewing mirror.'✶

'And we know how to get *up* to heaven, all right,' Angie put in. 'We just stand in front of a mirror and sing two verses from "Angels from the Realms of Glory" and our guardian angel will come and collect us.'

'Oooh,' Julia said. She thought for a moment. 'Could I come up with you, d'you think? I'd love to see heaven.'

'I wouldn't bother,' Gaby said. 'It's just clouds.'

'Clouds and angels,' said Angie.

'It sounds *lovely*,' Julia said. 'Please let me . . .'

Gaby shook her head. 'We'd better not. I think we're going to be in quite enough trouble about

✶ Every fifty years, angels are granted a look at earth through the magical viewing mirror. When our angels were looking through, it broke, and that's how they came to earth.

Sister Bertha, without taking you up to heaven as well.'

'Perhaps some other time,' Angie added politely.

Just then Marcy came in and glowered at the three of them gossiping together. 'What are you three plotting?' she asked sharply. 'Whenever I see you you're always whispering about something. What's the big secret?'

Julia looked innocent. 'We haven't got a secret!'

'Well, we *have* . . .' Angie said. 'It's –'

'Not a single secret! Not one!' Gaby burst out quickly, and suddenly a whole jam jar full of wild flowers collapsed and died.

The flowers were in Marcy's direct view. She stared at them and turned pale with surprise. 'Those . . . those flowers!' she said in a stunned voice. 'They were alive a few seconds ago, then they just crumpled and went brown. And now all the petals have fallen off!'

Julia guessed it had something to do with the angels. 'Things don't last long in here,' she said quickly. 'It's the central heating.'

'There isn't any central heating,' Marcy said, and she walked over to the dead flowers and looked at them in disbelief.

'Here today, gone tomorrow,' Gaby said cheerfully. 'It's like Sister Bertha, isn't it?'

Marcy's eyes narrowed. 'There's something odd about you two, I've always said it. You had something to do with these flowers dying and I bet you've got something to do with Sister Bertha's disappearance, too.'

'Us?' Gaby said. 'We're as innocent as . . . as . . .'

'As angels!' Angie said, and Gaby frowned at her.

Marcy moved very close to them, and Tiblet and Felix ran under the bed in fright. 'I'll be watching you two,' she said nastily. 'I'll be watching you every minute, and as soon as I discover what it is about you that's odd, I'm going to report it. It may take me a while, but I'll get there in the end.'

'If at first you don't succeed, fly, fly, fly again!' Angie said. 'That's what we say in he—'

Luckily, the bell went for supper, and Marcy, after a final glower at the three of them, went downstairs. Julia and the angels gave her time to get well ahead, then followed her down towards the dining hall. When they got to the door of the hall, though, they stopped.

'Who are all those men in black talking to the nuns?' Angie asked.

'That's the police,' Julia said.

Sarah came up behind them. 'They've come to start their investigations about Sister Bertha tonight,' she said. 'Isn't it exciting? They want to see us First Year girls immediately after supper.'

Gaby and Angie looked at each other.

'We'll have to go now!' Gaby angel-whispered.

'What, *now*? Before we've eaten?' Angie said.
'Couldn't we just have a quick –'⭐

'We can't have a quick anything!' Gaby said.
'Let's go!'

⭐ Angels love earth food. In heaven all they ever got
was milk and honey.

Julia stared at them, bemused. 'Are you talking to each other in your angel-speak?' she asked. 'What's happened?'

'What's happened is we're going to heaven and we're going right now!' Gaby said, and Angie just had time to squeal, 'Bye, Julia!' before Gaby rushed her out of the door.

5

Heaven in a Tizzy

The last few girls were going into the dining room as Gaby and Angie hurried in the opposite direction.

When they reached the bottom of the tower, Gaby released her wings. 'Come on,' she said, 'there's no one around. We'll fly up.'

'What's the big hurry?' Angie asked. 'Why do we have to miss supper?'

'Look,' Gaby said as they flitted up the stairwell of the tower. 'We've got to get up to heaven really quickly. We need to find Sister Bertha and get her back to earth before the police start their investigations.'

'We're not supposed to race around,' Angie said sternly. *Fret and hurry, rush and strife, Should not be an angel's life.*

'Halo Awareness Classes are all very well,' Gaby said, 'but they were for life in heaven. It's different down here. Now, flap your wings a bit harder and let's get a move on!'

Within a few seconds they were in their dorm, and a minute later they'd changed back into the

long nighties they'd been wearing when they'd arrived from heaven.

'Ready?' Gaby asked.

'Ready,' said Angie nervously. 'But I hope we're not going to get into awful trouble . . .'

'Oh, it'll be all right,' Gaby said comfortingly. 'Isn't there a little poem about it? I'm sure there must be one about angels going back to heaven – something like, *An angel returning to her cloud, Makes an Archangel shout out loud!* I just made that up! It's quite good, isn't it?'

'Sshhh!' Angie said, her teeth chattering from fright, 'we're getting too close. Someone in heaven will hear you!'

'Don't get so twitchy,' Gaby said. 'They'll just be pleased to see us back. Come on, let's stand in front of the mirror.'

The angels went into the bathroom and closed the door firmly behind them so that no one could wander in. They checked their nighties to make sure they were perfectly clear, patted their ringlets into place and folded their hands neatly in front of them. Then they looked into the mirror and started singing.

When they reached the end of the second verse of 'Angels from the Realms of Glory', a brilliant white light suddenly shone from out of the mirror. An instant later, a shimmering figure appeared, her vast gold and silver wings folded behind her.

'At last – Gabrielle and Angela!' the guardian angel said. 'The Archangel will be most pleased. You desireth to come back to your heavenly home, do you?'

'Yes, we do,' Gaby said humbly.

'If it pleases your Royal Angelness,' Angie added.

'Then – come forth!' said the guardian angel, and

a strange mist seemed to swirl out of the mirror and surround Gaby and Angie. It picked them up and swept them in. They felt a moment of extreme coldness, and the next thing they knew they were sitting on the edge of a cloud, swinging their feet.

They looked around them.

Gaby took a deep breath. 'Well, here we are, back in heaven,' she said.

'Easy as pie!' said Angie.

Gaby looked down to the cloud below, then right and left to the adjoining clouds. 'Well,' she said, 'things don't change much, do they?'

'Same old clouds,' Angie said. 'Still white, still fluffy, still –'

'*Boring.*'

Gaby was about to say more, when there was a beating of wings and a faint swirl of golden dust and the winged figure of the Archangel landed on the cloud next to them.

Both angels stood up immediately and bowed their heads, very much in awe of the Archangel, who was the greatest and most important angel on their level of heaven.

'Ah, my two runaway angels,' he said. 'You have returned to the fold. Welcome back to heaven, Level Six.'

Gaby and Angie gave a curtsy, their wing feathers quivering nervously.

'I am happy that you have seen the wrongness of your ways. Heaven rejoiceth when sheep returneth.'

'Yes, well, actually,' Gaby began, 'this may only be a temporary returneth of sheep.'

'What dost thou mean?'

'We've only come back to heaven to collect one of our teachers. She . . . er . . . arrived here by mistake.'

'Sister Bertha!' Angie put in eagerly. 'Have you seen her?'

The Archangel's serene expression changed and his eye started twitching. 'Aah,' he said. 'The lady in black. She ist . . . something to do with you, is she?'

'She's one of our nuns at school,' Gaby said. 'And really, it's not our fault that she's here, we were just helping a ghost.'

'Hmmm,' said the Archangel.

'Sister Bertha doesn't want to be here,' Gaby

went on earnestly, 'and they really need her on earth, so we'd like to take her back again, please.'

'And they need *us* back on earth, too,' Angie said, wanting to get this in as soon as possible. 'They need us to win the talent contest so that St Winifred's won't have to close.'

The Archangel, who didn't know what a talent contest was, so didn't have a clue what they were talking about, continued to look twitchy. 'The lady in black . . . so that ist how she cameth to be here,' he murmured. 'I wondered why she appeareth not on the forms sent up by Saint Peter.'

'So do you think we could take her back, then?' Gaby asked hopefully.

'Indeed, she should return,' said the Archangel, 'but you, my little angels, must stay.'

'But we –' Gaby began, and was stopped by a warning look from the Archangel.

'Perhaps, in the meantime, we could just go and see her?' Angie asked very nicely and politely indeed.

The Archangel pointed below them. 'Two clouds

downeth and three to the right,' he said. 'You cannot miss her.'

There was a sudden fanfare of trumpets.

'And now I must attendeth the golden trumpeters,' said the Archangel, 'but you will see me soon and I will decideth whether you should go down a level of heaven as punishment for all your naughty deeds.'

'Oh, please . . .' Gaby began, but there was just a rush of air as the Archangel's great wings flapped and carried him away.

Angie's bottom lip wobbled. 'I don't think he's going to let us go back to earth again.'

'Then we'll just have to get away on our own,' Gaby said.

'Oh, d'you really think we can?'

'We have to go back,' Gaby said. 'We promised Julia.'

'And angels *must* keep their promises,' Angie put in eagerly.

'As well as that, we've got save the school,' Gaby said. 'So that's decided then.' She ruffled Angie's wings. 'Cheer up. We'll find a way.' She stood on the edge of the cloud ready to launch herself off.' And now let's go and see Sister Bertha!'

The angels dived off and flew down and to the right. As they approached the cloud they saw a small black-robed figure in the centre of it, busily sweeping misty tufts of cloud into a pile.

Gaby and Angie hovered in the air for a while, watching her.

'What in heaven is she doing?' Angie asked.

Gaby shook her head, myst-ified, and then realised. 'Oh, she's cleaning up!' she said. 'She's tidying the cloud!'

As they watched, the

pile of fluffy cloud Sister Bertha had been working on tumbled over and fell off the edge. It immediately turned into rain and fell to earth.

A passing angel flew by, shaking her head. 'She's causing no end of fuss!' she said to Gaby and Angie. 'She won't stop interfering – polishing haloes, retuning harps, sweeping clouds up. Goodness knows what the weather's like down below with all the rain she's making!'

Gaby and Angie looked at each other.

'Oh dear,' Angie said. 'Heaven's in an uproar and it's all our fault! They'll never forgive us our trespasses!'

'Whatever *they* are,' said Gaby.

6

Round and Down the Rainbow

Gaby and Angie flew down and landed gently on the cloud next to Sister Bertha.

'Well,' she said, turning and looking them up and down. 'This is a fine carry on!'

'What's that?' Gaby asked.

'The state of this school – it's covered in fluff!'

'That's *cloud*,' Angie said.

'Cloud . . . fluff . . . call it what you like, it still needs clearing up.' She attacked a particularly wispy piece of cloud with the broom. 'And where *is* everyone? I haven't seen any of the Sisters for ages.

All I've seen is girls dressed up for the Nativity play. And they're all playing angels!'

She stopped sweeping for a moment and looked at them approvingly. 'Very good costumes, mind you. Did you get them from the dressing-up box?'

'No, we –' Angie began.

'We've had them for ages,' Gaby finished for her.

'Those wings,' Sister Bertha marvelled, 'look absolutely real.'

'That's because they –'

'That's because we look after them properly,' Gaby said swiftly.

Sister Bertha swept enthusiastically and another pile of cloud went over the edge and fell as rain.

'Can't you stop her?' The angel who had passed earlier was flying by again. 'Everyone's complaining. She never stops trying to organise us and she's eating us out of house and heaven – only this morning she drank twelve goblets of milk and honey.'

Gaby thought she looked like a friendly sort of angel so she flew up a little way to speak to her out of Sister Bertha's hearing.

'She's come from earth too soon,' Gaby explained, 'but we're trying to get her back again.'

'Back to earth?' the angel asked in amazement. 'Have you

been down to earth, then?'

Gaby nodded. 'And we want to go back there. Do you happen to know if the viewing mirror is being used at the moment?'

The angel shook her head.

'It's out of action. I heard that it's been sent to Level Nine for repairs.'

'Oh dear.' Gaby bit her lip worriedly. 'That means there's no way for us to get down to earth.'

'Unless . . .' said the angel.

'Unless what?'

'Well, I shouldn't really tell you this, but if it means getting rid of that little lady, then I will.'

'Is there a way, then?' Gaby asked breathlessly.

The angel nodded. 'I've heard – and it's only a rumour, mind – that you can go down the rainbow.'

'Down the rainbow? How do we do that?'

The angel's voice fell to a whisper. 'Well, I've never been there, of course, but word has it that if you go up . . . up . . . up higher than all heaven's levels, then you reach the back of beyond, where the rainbows start. There, in that special place, you can fly round the rainbow and slide down to earth.'

'Oh, wow!' Gaby said. 'Thank you very much.'

'Not at all,' said the angel, 'but I really don't want to be downgraded or have my harp taken away, so don't tell anyone I told you, will you?'

'Of course not!' Gaby said.

She flew down to Angie and Sister Bertha, and angel-whispered to Angie what she'd been told.

Angie looked at her with a mixture of nervousness and excitement. 'Now we know what to do, I think we'd better go straight away,' she said, 'before the Archangel finishes with his golden trumpeters and comes looking for us.'

'Just what I was thinking,' said Gaby. She looked at Sister Bertha. 'OK, then. You take one of her arms, I'll take the other.'

Lightly, delicately, they lifted Sister Bertha and began to fly upwards with her.

'What's happening?' Sister Bertha gasped. 'Are we flying?'

'That's right,' Gaby said soothingly. 'It's . . . er

. . . part of the Nativity play. All done with lines and pulleys.'

'Oooh!' squealed Sister Bertha, and she kicked out her feet so her habit billowed around her. 'What fun!'

Up and up, higher and higher, flew the angels. They passed strange lights and enchanted places, heard heavenly music and song, drifted by stars and planets, and reached levels of heaven they didn't know existed.

They flew upwards for seconds or minutes or days, they couldn't tell, until they reached a great plain of pale sky with no clouds at all. Above them was a strange glistening fog; a fog which sparkled and streamed and swirled in a never-ending kalei-doscope of colour.

Gaby gasped in wonder, looking at the glowing shades which danced and shifted and reflected on to her white nightie, turning it a hundred different glimmering colours. 'Red, orange, yellow, green blue, indigo, violet – rainbow colours!'

'We're at the very top of all the rainbows in the

world!' said an awestruck Angie. 'We're in a colour whirlpool!'

As for Sister Bertha, she'd long ago stopped talking; she was just speechless with wonder.

They hovered in one spot, looking down far, far below at the miles of rainbow unfurling.

'How do we know which way to slide?' Angie asked, for they were at the top arch of the rainbow, and of course it went in two directions.

Gaby shrugged. 'We don't, but somehow Sister Bertha needs to get back where she belongs, so we'll just have to keep thinking to ourselves, *St Winifred's*, and hope for the best.'

Angie moved towards the block of colour, and as she did so she lit up with shimmering rainbow hues. 'Shall we just sit on the top and push off, then?'

'I suppose so,' Gaby said, and she too moved nearer the rainbow and was taken up by its glowing colours.

They caught hold of Sister Bertha's habit and settled her at the top of the rainbow. 'Oh, I *am* enjoying myself!' she said. 'What's happening now?'

'We're taking you back to school,' Gaby said. She gave her a push. 'One, two,three and off you go!'

'Whee!!' cried Sister Bertha, and 'Whee!' cried the angels as they slid after her.

And as they did so, they thought to themselves, very determinedly, *St Winifred's*.

7

Mission Accomplished!

'Ouff!'

'Phew!'

Angie and Gaby landed on their own beds, flat on their backs.

Gaby lifted her head and stared around her. 'It's worked. We're back!'

'How strange!' said Angie. 'We seemed to be sliding for ever, but then as soon as we started off, we'd arrived!' She looked across the room. 'And Sister Bertha's back, too!'

Sister Bertha was lying on Julia's bed in a heap of

black draperies, breathing deeply.

'Hurry,' Gaby said to Angie. 'Let's get changed before she recovers!' And they quickly took off their nighties, tucked their wings under their vests and put on their school uniforms.

'What are we going to say to Sister Bertha?' Angie said breathlessly. 'How are we going to explain?'

'We won't have to say a word because she won't remember anything about it,' Gaby said. 'People never do – didn't you know? That's the first rule of being sent to heaven before your time.'

They stood at the foot of Julia's bed and waited for Sister Bertha to catch her breath and sit up. It was another minute before she did so.

'Good heavens!' she said then, and Gaby and Angie hid a giggle at her choice of words. 'I must have dropped off.'

'That's right – dropped right off the edge of a rainbow!' Gaby angel-whispered.

'Fancy me falling asleep like that. I must have been really tired. But what are you two girls doing? What time is it?'

Gaby was just going to say that she didn't know, when Nicola burst in and started rummaging in her locker.

'Come on,

you two! Supper time!' she said. 'Didn't you hear the bell?'

'Supper time,' Gaby angel-whispered, 'but supper time, what day?'

'And – guess what?' Nicola went on. 'The police are here to start their investigations.'

Gaby and Angie looked at each other in amazement: they'd arrived back on earth at practically the same time as they'd left! Only a few moments had gone by since they'd been standing outside the dining room with Julia.

'They're going to question us tower dorm girls first,' Nicola said, straightening up from her locker, 'and then look in Sister Bertha's room for . . .' she looked across the beds and gave a short scream. 'Sister Bertha!'

'Yes, dear?' said the good lady.

'You're missing!'

'Am I?' Sister Bertha looked down at herself. 'I don't appear to be. Which bits?'

'But . . . but . . .'

'We just got here and found Sister Bertha on the

bed,' Gaby said truthfully.

'Yes, and I've had a lovely sleep.' She beamed at everyone. 'I dreamt of angels . . .'

Angie smiled sweetly. 'How lovely. What could be nicer?'

'But I don't understand,' Nicola said in a stunned voice. 'Where has she been all this time?'

Gaby made for the door. 'I think we'd better all go down to supper,' she said. 'If people think you're missing, Sister Bertha, then we ought to let them see that you're *not*.'

Sister Bertha had been greeted with delight by the staff and girls of St Winifred's, the police had been dismissed, and it was generally agreed that she must have had some sort of memory loss.

Julia, of course, couldn't wait to get the angels in a corner of the common room after supper . . .

'Have you been? Have you really been there?' she asked.

'Course!' Gaby said.

'Mission accomplished!' added Angie.

'But you were only away a minute! You just dis-appeared and I'd hardly turned away before you were back again.'

Gaby and Angie looked vague. 'Time's different up there,' Gaby said.

'But why?'

'Why? Angie said. 'We don't know. *Angels never asketh why, Angels just sing and fly!*'

'Fancy,' said Julia, shaking her head in puzzle-ment.

Sarah stood up and turned off the television so that everyone had to pay attention. The angels, who loved everything and anything on TV, pulled faces.

'Now, we've got a couple of things we need to talk about,' Sarah said. 'First, has anyone got any ideas about Sister Bertha? She couldn't possibly have been in our dorm all that time.'

'No. Where *has* she been?' asked Susie.

'How come she can't remember anything?' Nicola put in.

'I think the police ought to have stayed and

asked questions,' Marcy said darkly. She stared at
Gaby and Angie. 'I think those who found her
know a bit more than they're saying . . .'

'Perhaps she just fell asleep somewhere . . . in a
cupboard?' Julia suggested.

'Perhaps she was kidnapped by aliens!' Susie
joked.

'What's aliens?' Angie wanted to know.

'Oh, you know, like on that TV programme —
people from outer space,' Susie explained.

'Is heaven outer space?' Angie asked.

'Yes, I suppose so,' said Susie.

'Then *we're* aliens,' Angie said happily.

Gaby gave her a sharp nudge in the ribs. "Course we're not.'

'We are!'

Some of the other First Years looked at Angie curiously.

'She means because . . . er . . . earth is spinning in space, then we're all from outer space so we're all aliens,' Julia said.

'No, I don't,' Angie said. 'I mean that me and Gaby are aliens because we're –'

'Hedgehogs!' Gaby suddenly shouted.

The room went silent and everyone looked at her.

'You're . . . *hedgehogs*?' Sarah said. 'What d'you mean?'

'There are hedgehogs just outside the window. Foraging for food. You look!' Gaby blustered, for she was sitting on the window sill and had heard a mother and two baby hedgehogs outside, talking about the lack of worms for supper. ✻

The girls ran to the window and flung it open. Sure enough, three hedgehogs scuttled away under the bushes.

'But, Gaby, how did you know they were there?' Sarah asked.

'I . . . er . . .' Gaby floundered, and frowned at Angie for getting her into this spot, '. . . saw

✻ Because angels' ears are so finely tuned to animal language, they can hear really tiny sounds.

66

them earlier – I just remembered them.' As she spoke, a small pot of African violets suddenly keeled over.

A bit later, when everyone had got over the hedgehogs and forgotten about the aliens business,

Sarah began again.

'So no one's got any ideas about Sister Bertha, then?'

'What I want to know,' Marcy said, jabbing a finger at the angels, 'is how come whenever there's some sort of funny business, *they're* involved.'

'Don't be silly,' Julia said. 'They just happened to be upstairs, that's all. Nicola was up there as well.'

'Anyway,' Sarah said, 'she's back and that's that, and we'll leave it to the Sisters to work out where she's been. But now that we haven't got her to worry about, perhaps we all ought to help Gaby and Angie with the singing contest. Now, you two, have you decided what song to sing?'

'Sister Anne spoke to us at supper,' Gaby said. 'She wants us to do the song we learnt at the beginning of term – the world in harmony one.'

'*Birds and beasts, men and mice!*' Angie trilled the first line and Marcy made an exaggerated sick noise.

'Be quiet, Marcy!' Sarah said. 'I know it's a bit

sweet, but that's just the sort of thing that wins in these contests. If Gaby and Angie are going to save St Winifred's, then the sweeter the better!'

Everyone started talking excitedly then about television cameras coming to the school – apart from Angie, who stared at the television set for some time and then asked Gaby, 'So what happens? Do they sort of make us smaller and squash us in the back of the set? And suppose they can't make us big again?'

'Sshh!' Gaby said. 'It's all *electrical*. They kind of photograph us and then it goes out on the airwaves.'

'I don't understand. What d'you mean?'

'Oh, I don't know,' Gaby said impatiently. 'It's just some sort of magic.'

'Oh, right. Same as *we're* a bit magic,' said Angie.

Marcy Investigates

A week later, up in the dorm, Angie tugged at Julia's hand. 'I want to clean my teeth,' she said. 'Will you come into the bathroom with me?'

'If you like,' Julia said. 'But that's four times you've cleaned them today.'

'That's because I want my teeth to *gleam* when we're on television.'

'That's all very well,' Julia said, 'but are you going to have someone with you in front of mirrors for *ever*?'

'Probably not for *ever*,' Angie replied, 'but just

for now we'd better.'

Gaby nodded. 'The Archangel will be furious with us for disappearing again. He's going to seize the first chance he can to appear in a mirror and try and get us back to heaven.'

'But he won't appear if there's a human around, will he?' Angie put in a bit fearfully.

'Of course not,' Gaby said, but she looked over her shoulder doubtfully as she spoke. She actually thought she'd seen the shadowy form of the Archangel appearing in one of the wardrobe mirrors only that morning, but she didn't want to tell Angie because she knew she'd get into a terrible state.

Julia jumped off her bed. 'Well, we'd better not take any chances,' she said, 'not with the contest tomorrow. Suppose he whisked you back so you couldn't enter!'

'Then we wouldn't win the money and St Winifred's would be closed and it would all be heaven's fault!' Gaby said.

Julia and Angie went into the bathroom and

Gaby heard the sound of enthusiastic teeth-cleaning. Suddenly there was a yowl from outside and Felix shot through the door saying that Marcy was coming up the stairs. A moment later she stomped in, driving both cats under the bed.

'Just the person I want to see,' she said to Gaby. 'I'm doing a spot of investigating.'

'What sort of investigating?' Gaby asked, feeling her wing feathers begin to prickle with fright.

'Oh, just looking into certain things for the school magazine.'

'We haven't got a school magazine.'

'We have now,' Marcy said, 'because I've started one. I'm writing about unexplained mysteries. Mysteries like how you and Angie seem to know things before anyone else.' She narrowed her eyes. 'And how you sometimes arrive at places before anyone else, too.'

'Oh, we've always been fast on our feet,' Gaby said. She smiled sweetly. 'We're always flying here, there and everywhere!'

'Hmm,' said Marcy thoughtfully. *'Flying here,*

there and everywhere,' she repeated, and she wrote it down in her notebook. Gaby wondered if she'd gone too far.

'The other thing I've been looking into,' Marcy went on, 'is where Sister Bertha could have gone when she was missing. I've just been talking to her, you see.'

'Have you really?' said Gaby, trying to look unconcerned.

'She's very muddled. She can't remember where she's been, but she said she had lots of dreams about clouds – great big fluffy clouds.'

'Clouds!' Angie said, coming back from the bathroom. 'Don't talk to me about clouds! I was pleased to see the back of –'

'Marcy's trying to find out where Sister Bertha could have gone,' Gaby said quickly.

Marcy looked from Gaby to Angie and back again. 'Sister Bertha told me that she feels different. More serene and spiritual, she put it – as if she's been in a very quiet and peaceful place.'

'Well, that's all right then,' Gaby said. 'So

73

wherever she went, it must have done her good.'

'But where *was* that?' Marcy said. 'That's what I want to know. And what did you two have to do with it?'

'Oh, honestly,' Julia interrupted, 'what does it matter? Sister Bertha's been away, and now she's back.'

'Because if it *was* discovered that you two were

mixed up in it, I bet you wouldn't be allowed to be in the contest . . .'

Gaby and Angie looked at each other, worried, but Julia, who was looking out of the dorm window, suddenly gave a start. 'There's a great big silver van coming down the drive!' she shouted. 'The television people have arrived!'

Gaby, thankful for the interruption, grabbed Angie's hand and ran to the door. 'Come on,' she said, 'it's nearly time for us to be stars. Let's go!'

9

TV Stars

'All we've got to hope,' Gaby said to Angie in bed early the next morning, 'is that Marcy doesn't discover too much with her investigations.'

As Angie stretched, one of her wings popped out of her nightie. 'At least not before we've been on TV,' she said, sitting up and carefully tucking it back in. 'Now, what are we wearing?'

'School uniform,' Gaby said promptly. 'Mother Superior said we have to.'

'Have you got a clean shirt?'

''Course I have!'

Gaby and Angie had run through their chosen song about twenty times the previous afternoon, and they'd also done sound tests and time checks and all sorts of other technical trials. They were going to be filmed at six o'clock that evening. It would go out live on TV, and they'd be the eighth act to appear in the contest. When all twelve had performed their songs, the panel of judges back in the television studio would select the winner.

That morning in the dining hall practically everyone in the school had come up to wish Gaby and Angie good luck. St Winifred's might be a funny old school, but none of the girls wanted it to close, because then they'd have to go to an ordinary school, a *proper* school.

In the afternoon, the floor manager of the television unit sent for Gaby and Angie to run some more tests.

Mr Ritchie was a big, rather worried-looking man wearing a baseball cap. He moved Gaby and Angie around the stage in the hall, undecided about where they should stand.

'Everything's got to be exactly right,' he said.
'This is my first job on my own and I want it to be
perfect.'

Gaby and Angie, humming their song under
their breath, moved around, eager to please.

'You just look a bit . . . wooden,' Mr Ritchie
said. He looked at them consideringly. 'Got it!' he
said. 'What you need is a gimmick!'

'Thanks, but we've already eaten,' Angie said
politely.

'You've got lovely voices, no doubt about that,' Mr Ritchie went on, 'but you need some sort of device to make you stand out from the other acts. Now, what is it you remind me of . . .' He frowned deeply and then shouted, 'I've got it – angels!'

Gaby and Angie started visibly.

'Angelic voices, golden curls, sweet smiles . . . yeah, you look just like angels!'

'Er, no, I don't think so,' Angie said, and Gaby tried to pull a face and make herself look ugly.

'You're right, Rich!' one of the other TV men agreed.

'All they need is a harp,' someone else shouted.

'I think,' said Mr Ritchie, 'that we ought to dress you up as angels!'

'Oh crumbs,' Gaby angel-whispered, 'this is a bit too close for comfort.'

Angie stood quaking, desperately trying to think of the most unangelic thing she could do to put Mr Ritchie off the idea. All she could think of, though, was picking her nose – and she couldn't bring herself to do that.

'Yeah, we'll deck you out in long nighties and make you some wings and haloes! It'll be a winner!'

'I suppose,' Gaby – who was *very* keen to be a TV star – angel-whispered to Angie, 'that we could go along with it. We'll be really different from everyone else, and it's bound to get us a few more points with the judges.'

'What's more, we know we can really play our parts well!' said Angie.

Gaby smiled sweetly at Mr Ritchie. 'It sounds good to us,' she said. 'One thing though; there are lots of clothes in the dressing-up basket here – and . . . er . . . we'd like to sort out our own wings.'

'Sure thing.' Mr Ritchie clapped his hands. 'OK, let's get this show on the road. Get moving, you crew!' he said. 'And another thing – the song is all about harmony in the world, animals and humans getting on together and all that stuff, so how about getting a couple of animals in to sit by these girls while they're singing?'

'Too difficult, boss,' one of his men said. 'Animals take months of training.'

Gaby and Angie winked at each other. 'Leave that to us,' Gaby said.

A couple of hours later, when school was over for the day, Gaby and Angie came out of the hall wearing their special new angel outfits. The first person they saw was Julia.

'What d'you think you're doing?' she shrieked. 'You mustn't let people see you dressed like that! Go upstairs and change immediately!'

Gaby giggled. 'No, no, it's OK!' she said. 'The TV man wants us dressed like this.'

'Like angels?!'

Gaby and Angie nodded.

'Oh my goodness! What if anyone . . .'

A few other First Year girls came up and looked them over admiringly, and then Marcy turned up.

'Angels!' she said. 'Angels! Well, what a strange coincidence.'

'What d'you mean?' Gaby asked.

'I've been speaking to Sister Bertha again – for the magazine, you know. She still doesn't know

where she went when she disappeared, but she's remembered more dreams that she had.' Marcy paused. 'Beautiful dreams about angels.'

'Well, that is a coincidence,' Gaby said. 'But you'll have to excuse us now.' She set off down the corridor with Angie in pursuit behind her. 'We've just got to go and collect a few animals.'

'D'you think we can have tigers?' Angie asked as they ran.

10

Angels' Delight

It was almost six o'clock. Angie and Gaby were in their places on the stage, surrounded by cameras and microphones and pieces of TV equipment.

Behind them stood a large harp (a last-minute addition ordered by Mr Ritchie) and in front of them was an array of animals: a mouse, two hedgehogs, a fox, Stanley the gardener's dog, Felix and Tiblet, three rabbits and two white doves. Angie hadn't found any tigers so had come back with a cow instead, but Mr Ritchie had told her there was no room for it.

The animals had been given a quiet talking-to by the angels, who'd explained to them that it was very, very important that they all appeared to get on, just for a couple of hours. Gaby had also given them a bit of a fright by saying that if the school closed, there was no saying what could happen – that blocks of flats might be built over the entire site and then they'd all lose their homes.

So the scene was set: our angels were radiant and glorious, the animals were fluffy, cute and *very* well-behaved, and Mr Ritchie was almost beside himself with bossiness and self-importance.

The entire school was allowed in to watch the filming. The nuns were sitting at the back of the stage (Mr Ritchie felt it would add a little extra *something* to the proceedings if the odd nun or two were to be seen in the background), and the First Year girls were in the front row of the hall. Marcy was sitting as close to the stage as it was possible to get and looking at the angels through suspicious, narrowed eyes.

Six o'clock arrived, and on the TV monitor at the side of the stage, everyone was able to see the acts going out live from the other schools. Angie and Gaby watched intently.

'Not being boastful,' Angie angel-whispered, 'because *Angels shouldn't brag and boast, But always take a modest post* – but none of them are as good as us.'

'We'll win it. It's a piece of angel cake!' said Gaby.

At last it was their turn.

'And now we go live to St Winifred's School –

Gabrielle and Angela: the two angels!' said the announcer.

Gaby and Angie started singing as beautifully as ever, their only accompaniment the soft cooing of the doves, who rose to flutter over them. Mr Ritchie, the technicians, Mother Superior and the whole school watched, enthralled, as they went through the first verse of their song.

And then, off camera, there was a yell from Mr Ritchie, who was wearing headphones which connected him with the main studio.

'Something's gone wrong!' he called. 'The girls aren't coming out on the screens!'

Every eye shot across to the TV

monitor. Sure enough, the harp was there, the animals were there, the doves were cooing above – but on the TV screen there was absolutely no sign of Gaby and Angie.

'Carry on! Carry on!' Mr Ritchie gestured to the angels. 'We'll try and fix it!'

Gaby and Angie sang on.

Mr Ritchie was turning red. 'I'll get sacked for this! I'll never work again!' he raged, storming about. 'I can't understand what's gone wrong!'

In the middle of the song there was a pause when the angels were supposed to bend down and talk to the animals.

Angie picked Stanley up to pet him – and of course it looked on the TV monitor as if the dog was flying through the air. 'What do you think's going wrong?' she angel-whispered to Gaby.

'Don't know!' Gaby said, holding up the fox. But then she suddenly had an idea. 'Unless, of course, it's something to do with us being angels. *Real* angels. Maybe we don't appear on film because we're not really *live on earth*.'

'What?!'

But there was no time to say anything else because they had to put down the animals and go into the second half of the song.

Mr Ritchie was now puce with rage and frustration, blaming the weather, the filming, the cameraman, the school and electrical currents by turn.

The angels finished their song. There was a burst of applause from the hall, but Mr Ritchie looked as though he was going to turn a somersault with sheer anger.

Suddenly, though, his face cleared.

'I see,' he said into a portable telephone. 'Thanks, sir. Yes, I thought it was a good idea, too.'

As the TV monitor began showing another act from the next school, Mr Ritchie came to the front of the stage, beaming widely.

'My editor in the studio thinks I deliberately fixed it so that the angels wouldn't appear on film! He said angelic voices appearing out of nowhere was the best gimmick he'd ever heard of in his life!'

The angels and everyone else breathed a sigh of relief.

'But how could that happen?' one of the technicians called out.

'The whole thing's ridiculous!' said Sister Gertrude, the Maths teacher.

'Strangest thing I ever heard in my life!' someone else said, and there were other murmurings of disbelief.

Marcy's voice rose above everyone else's. 'Shouldn't it be *investigated*?' she said, but everyone was too excited to pay much attention to her, and anyway, they wanted to watch the acts from the other schools on the TV monitor.

When all the acts had finished and were being judged, Mother Superior came up, congratulated Angie and Gaby on their performance and said if they ever wanted someone to accompany them on the tambourine, she'd be pleased to consider it.

Sister Bertha came over, looking thoughtful.

'Beautiful, girls,' she said. 'Absolutely heavenly.'

'Thank you, Sister Bertha,' Gaby and Angie chorused.

'You *do* remind me of someone I saw recently. I just can't think who . . . or where . . .'

Marcy seemed to appear out of nowhere. 'The school magazine will be most interested if you ever *do* remember, Sister Bertha,' she said.

As Gaby and Angie nudged each other, Mr Ritchie suddenly let up a whoop of glee. 'You've won!' he yelled. 'St Winifred's have won the contest! Our angels got the maximum possible number of points!'

Of course, the whole school went mad after this, and for at least ten minutes no one could make themselves heard.

When everyone had hugged and kissed everyone else, though, and Sister Gertrude had worked out that with the prize money St Winifred's could keep

going for at least another two years, there was a moment's calm and everyone paused for breath. In the silence could be heard a few *wuffs* from Stanley and a long, long, plaintive mew from Tiblet.

Sister Bertha smiled sweetly. 'I do think we ought to let the animals go outside now,' she said. 'Stanley is complaining he's been cooped up quite long enough and Tiblet says her supper is waiting in the kitchen.'

Marcy's jaw dropped and she reached for her notebook. Everyone else turned to stare at Sister Bertha in amazement.

'Oh!' Sister Bertha said, clapping her hand to her mouth. 'Where on earth did I learn that?'

No one said anything.

'I think she means,' Angie angel-whispered, 'where in *heaven* did she learn that?'

'Well,' Gaby said, 'let's hope she doesn't ever remember!'